SILENT VOICES

Fran Lewis

Silent Voices

Copyright © Fran Lewis, 2019

ISBN: 978-1-948638-24-1

Printed in the United States of America

First Edition, June 2019

Cover Design by Genevieve Scholl
Edited by Genevieve Scholl
Formatted by Genevieve Scholl

TABLE OF CONTENTS

REVIEW BY JAN HOLIDAY

Silent Voices speak from the grave in this gothic style collection of short stories by *Fran Lewis.*
If you ever felt wrong and thought of revenge, one of these characters in
Silent Voices could do the job and do it well. And you might find you agree with me that some of the characters deserve what they get.
The atmosphere and characters feel real in these stories and you are drawn in to see what happens next. At times I was there with them in their *GRAVES.* I read the whole book in two short sittings.
Fran Lewis is one of my go-to authors for great short stories. As a short story writer and reader myself, I was fascinated by the fabulous imagery in this collection.
You will be enthralled by *Fran Lewis'* talent. **My Grandmother** is my favorite. This grandmother outwits her three granddaughters and they don't see it coming.

You can find more stories like these in Fran's other books; **Faces Behind the Stones, Bad Choices and Hidden Truths & Lies.** Enjoy this read!

Faces Behind the Stones
https://www.amazon.com/gp/product/1937593967

Bad Choices: Faces Behind the Stones (Volume

2) Paperback
https://www.amazon.com/gp/product/1938243773

Hidden Truths & Lies (Faces Behind the Stones)
https://www.amazon.com/Hidden-Truths-Faces-Behind-Stones/dp/1604149124/

REVIEW BY KAREN VAUGHAN, AUTHOR OF DEAD TO WRITES

"Once again Ms. Lewis has a hit with her series … Silent Voices is a surefire hit!

The most chilling of her stories to date!!!"

REVIEW BY ANN STANMORE

"Fran Lewis' latest in the Silent Voices series reveals more of the dark side of human nature.
Fran has again used her skills to both entertain, thrill and shock yet at the same time arouse a somewhat reluctant sympathy. Not for the faint hearted."

DEDICATION

These stories might be fiction, but the first two are based on real life situations. I want to dedicate this book to my grandmother Katie Goldberg, who shared her story with me, and my grandmother Bertha, who I really never got to know. I want to thank my cousins Hedy Braverman, Stacy Modlin, and Eunice Pasher for their input on the story titled Bertha.

INTRODUCTION

Driving down a rocky road, I saw the overgrown grass, weeds, and poison ivy overtaking the perimeter of the bushes. The smell of mildew permeated the air, along with the stench of animals, killed by cars, coming up from the ground along this dirt road. I could see the sadness on the faces in the cars behind me; I could feel the pain and sorrow.

As I looked inside the cars and saw the faces of the drivers, I began to wonder what they were thinking, their thoughts and feelings as they traveled down life's highway, maybe for the very last time. What stories lay behind the faces at the wheel of each oncoming car? What stories were hidden?

Faces: So many stories. Silent Voices.

Here are seven stories that will bring chills down your spine and make you wonder: what lies behind the stones? Who lives here? Each voice you will hear has been silenced by the evil of others. Rosie and many others in the camps were tortured and enslaved, and not allowed to speak out at all. Bertha's voice was never heard by her aunt, who used her to cook, clean, and even service men for money. Next is a teacher who believed that children should be seen and not ever heard, and their opinions were off limits. Sarah Jones knew the secret that her cousin Benita was hiding, and what she had done to her own mother. Sarah would bide her time and take on not only Benita but others, too. This is the story of how Sarah Jones decided to fight back. But did she succeed?

Finally, there are several who have wronged so many, and these last three remain behind stones that barely stand straight, where their names are engraved but covered with mud and soil, so that no one will ever give them the honor of saying a prayer over them or mourning their deaths. These three come from different walks of life: one is a lawyer, another an accountant, and the third a judge. What are they guilty of? Read their stories as they tell them, and you decide if their fates were just or not, as they blackmailed and threatened so many whose voices, you'll learn, were silenced in fear.

Within this world there are many who gain wealth by taking what belongs to others.

ROSIE'S WORDS: I DID SURVIVE!

As I lay here in my coffin, I wanted to tell my story in my own words before I can no longer speak.

My name is Rosie, and my parents were Bella and Joseph. My life turned into a nightmare one morning while going, along with my sisters, to do some chores for my parents. Walking to the local market to get the necessary ingredients that my mom needed to bake some bread, we were accosted by some men, placed in a truck, and covered with some type of tarp. No one saw us, as the streets were quiet that early in the morning, and we were too terrified to scream. All my life I had always been happy, and my sisters and I loved being together. We got along except for the usual sisterly arguments about borrowing clothes, shoes, or boys. But on that warm and sunny morning, a black cloud would shroud all of us. The fear that was in our hearts could be seen on each of our faces. Never had we expected what would be our lives for so long.

The men taped our mouths and placed something over our heads so we could not see. I counted the minutes in my head, and feared for our lives.

When the truck came to a halt, we were dragged out, thrown on the dirty ground, and warned not to move an inch. When we were finally allowed to see the light, we were standing in front of a gate that was marked with the name of a place I won't even utter. Separated from my sisters and placed in a cold, muddy cell with nothing more than a flimsy dress, water that looked dirty, and with no air or vent, I sat down in the corner of the room and cried—alone, fearful, and not knowing why I was there. I tried listening at the door that was bolted shut, to hear if I could understand what my captors wanted from me and my sisters. I had no idea if they were alive or dead. That was the beginning of my nightmare that would last for months, or maybe even years. I lost track of the time.

Doctors are supposed to save lives, not destroy them. I was placed in a cell that was filthy, with rodents crawling from all sections, as there were so many holes inside it. There were no windows, no vents, just a small metal opening in the door to push food through—food that I would rarely touch, because just smelling it allowed me to know that it was drugged and would make me even sicker than I already was.

My cot had a small mattress, a small pillow, and a blanket with holes in it. The cell was about four feet long and six feet wide. The bars on the door were so close together I could barely see outside, but the screams and cries of the others could not be ignored. Fear entered my heart, as I had no idea what they were going to do to me or why.

It was the time period of the Third Reich, and the Nazi doctors violated more than my privacy and dignity—they tore at my inner core and soul. They were cruel, relentless, and heartless, and demanded total submission. They taunted us every chance they got, and the tortures were many.

One morning, after trying to make me eat what was supposed to pass for oatmeal—but looked like someone's stomach contents—they took me into a stark white lab and placed a burning hot sun lamp on my lower parts. They did that many times, and the pain was horrific. My screams were unheard, and the faces of those in the room were frightening, as they just smiled, laughed, and wrote down what they saw. It only took about twenty minutes for all the people inside to die when cremated. They were taken into the crematorium and burned, and then their ashes were thrown into a coffin. Any bones or residue was just thrown on the ground. Those that survived lived with their torment for years to come, and had many sleepless nights.

***

Remarkably, there were instances of individual resistance and collective efforts at fighting back inside Auschwitz. Poles, Communists, and other national groups established networks in the main camp. A few Jews escaped from Birkenau, and there were recorded assaults on Nazi guards even at the entrance to the gas chambers.

The "Sonderkommando" revolt in October 1944 was the extraordinary example of physical resistance. Of those who received numbers at Auschwitz-Birkenau, only 65,000 survived. It is estimated that only about 200,000 people who passed through all the Auschwitz camps survived. Historians and analysts estimate the number of people murdered at Auschwitz was somewhere between 2.1 million and 4 million, of whom the vast majority were Jews. Unfortunately, their prisoner numbers were burned into their arms. Many hid them when this was over, not wanting the world to know what they'd endured.

***

Every day was worse than the one before, and I feared I would soon be one of those thrown into the burning inferno, and then into a hole with the rest of the bodies. The heartless b...... that these less than human captors were was frightening, and the heart palpitations came more frequently. It took every ounce of thought and energy to calm myself down.

I endured many indignities, and so many horrific moments lying exposed on a table, held with restraints, the cold metal like ice attached to my bare skin. The men who performed these experiments, and the nurses that accompanied them, were cruel and heartless, and their evil countenances resonated. They flaunted their air of superiority, ridding the world of what they claimed were inferior classes, or women who might give birth to children greater than their own. Fear was in my heart as they stared at me, and I prayed that they would forget that I was even there as the chills ran down my spine from their cold stares. I lived each day not knowing if I'd make the next. My skin browned, my eyes became sallow, and my body looking skeletal as I prayed each day to end my misery.

One night, back in my barracks with so many others, I heard voices outside and wondered what they had planned. I knew from hearing the guards talking when they thought we could not hear them—or were asleep on the cold floors that were our beds, with nothing to cover us but some old smelly sheets or blankets—that they believed the Allies were coming, and all of us might be sent to our deaths before our captors fled.

What happened next is just what I recall, but it could have happened another way so please don't hold me to my account. Several men came into our barracks, covered us with warm blankets, and gave us water to drink, and gestured that we stay quiet. Not moving a muscle and not knowing who they were, or if we could trust them, I prayed that I would make it out and never return. My sisters were somewhere, and I had no idea where.

The face of someone I realized I knew was hidden by a hat covering his head, just letting his deep blue eyes shine through. I whispered, "Max," and he gestured, letting me know that he was there to rescue us. The next thing I knew, I was outside, going into an underground tunnel, hoping that at the other end I would see the sunshine. The tunnel was dark and dank, and smelled of dead animals and rot, but for now it was like a palace that would bring me to freedom.

When we finally came to the end of the tunnel, we were placed in a truck, covered over by a tarp so no one would see us, and then taken to a house with a family that would care for us until we could be moved once again. These people might have been Germans, but they cared for us, gave us food and clothing, and did not say much at all. For the first time, I felt safe; but for how long?

But not everything went smoothly. Just as we were about to find our way out, and hoping that Max would come and save us from the hell we were still reliving, someone came to the house where we were hiding and tried to enter and search for prisoners that might have escaped from the camp. Fanny and I searched around for somewhere to hide. We found an opening in the floor that led to a hidden cellar, and prayed that we would be able to climb down, not make any noise, and not be found out. That would not only end our lives, but those of the people that were hiding us. We hoped that no one would hear us and that Max would eventually return.

With little air, just enough water for about two or three days, and a limited amount of food stored in the cellar, we were about to give up when someone came down the ladder. Hoping it was Max, we did not reveal ourselves. Whispering our names and hoping we were down there, Max appeared as promised. But, the road to freedom still had many obstacles, as we had to manage to leave this house unseen.

In the dead of the night, in freezing temperatures and with the snow coming down, wearing whatever these people could find to keep us warm, we entered what was to be our passage to freedom, an underground tunnel. As we entered the tunnel, voices were heard that belonged to a group of men. We would never know their names, but their goal was to get us to safety somehow.

Days passed—weeks—and then, finally, the light before the dark appeared once again as we traveled in the darkness and made our way to Switzerland. Max was our savior. Then, with the help of so many more people whose faces were all a blur, I wound up on Ellis Island in America. Where would I go from there? What would my destiny be? I didn't care. I just knew that I was finally safe from those monsters.

But now I had to learn my real fate. What had they done to me? How would the x-rays and what they did to me change my life? How could I ever forget?

Leaving the horrors behind would only bring new ones. When I entered Ellis Island, I prayed for my safety and my sanity. The horrors inflicted on me and so many others could not be denied, although no one ever really understood my fear of the dark, being alone, or even going to the doctor's office. When I accidentally burned my hand when the grease spattered while cooking, I feared going to the doctor, and refused to allow them to take me there. The metal table, the instruments, brought back memories, and I told them to bring me something from the pharmacy that would help heal my burn.

I still trembled at the sight of anyone

coming close to me. I had nightmares about what was done to me. Now I was safe, but I never really felt safe. I hoped to be reunited with my sisters and Max, who would continue to play an important role in my life. I was convinced, by Max and others, that I needed some medical attention due to the physical and mental abuse I had received. My physical condition was poor when I arrived in the United States, and I had to have many tests, exams, and determinations to find out just how the Nazis' treatment of me would affect me in the future. Some of the torture I remembered, and others I chose to forget. Every day I found myself dealing with stomach problems, headaches, and pain everywhere; real or imagined, I didn't know. At times, I saw myself on that cold metal table, saw the horrific faces of those monsters, and heard the screams of so many who were about to be slaughtered.

Going through Ellis Island and hoping they would allow me to enter America was a blur in my mind. The fear that they would send me back was always on my mind. Learning to trust my new country would take time and patience on the part of so many people. Would I ever really be free? What would my freedom be like in this new world?

Getting to know more about my new surroundings, trying to walk long distances was hard, as my eyes seemed blurred and I could not see clearly. Later, I would learn the definition of cataracts, but I still didn't understand how or why I'd gotten them.

Long nights, hard days, and some time passed before I felt safe walking on the streets. But my eyes were so bad that in order to get anywhere, I either needed someone with me or I had to count the steps to wherever I was going, hoping to get to my destination without having to cross many streets. I could not see the colors of the street lights, but I knew which one was green by where it was on the lighted lamp; or I would ask someone to cross me.

Fanny and Max found each other and were married months after our escape. Things were great for quite some time, and they had five beautiful children to care for, nurture, and love. I was an aunt. But life brought other hardships and strife. When Fanny was about to give birth to child number six, she developed pneumonia and she and the baby died in childbirth, leaving Max alone with five children ages twelve to two. How would he handle this, and how would he continue to support his family without a wife to care for them?

Max struggled for a long time, until he decided to make a life changing choice. Having to work, he needed someone to care for his children, and that meant taking a new wife. Shondina, Tillie, and I were the logical choices, as we were the aunts of his five children. Getting to know each one of us, he realized that I would be a perfect fit, but would his children accept me? Becoming his wife was fine, but understanding and fulfilling my duties as a wife would take time.

I still woke up in the middle of the night and thought I was back in that room on that metal cot, with those evil eyes staring at me. I yelled and screamed, and I didn't think I would ever be the same, even with my family and my husband Max helping and guiding me every single day. His children did not really accept me as their parent after their real mother passed away in childbirth, and their father needed someone to step in and take care of them.

Life had not been easy for me, and at times, I felt that I had been trapped in another type of prison since coming to America. I loved being with Max and his family, but the children still had a long way to go to realize that I was not trying to take the place of their mother. I was just hoping to be a part of their lives.

I might be gone, telling you this story from behind a stone in a cemetery, but I hope that what I continued to deal with will help people realize that these events did happen, and that they will never forget. I'm not sure if I was ever free. For my whole life married to Max I was blessed, and his/my children were the biggest blessings in my life. But things never really went smoothly, and freedom was something I don't think I ever felt at any point.

When I passed, Max found a red case with a lock on it, which I had carried with me wherever I went. At home, it was under my bed, and no one ever knew what was in it or why I was so protective of the contents. When Max opened it after my passing, there was note that I'd had one of my children— which one I will not say—write for me, as I could not read or write. The note stated what was in the box, what was to be done with it, and why I never learned to trust those that were not under my own roof. Freedom; I still don't know if I will ever be free!

BERTHA: A YOUNG GIRL'S NIGHTMARE

My name on the next stone is hard to read, as the stone is quite old. I never wanted a fanfare when I left this world, but there are many reasons why my life was hard, and why I never really enjoyed each day of my life living in America. I loved living in Russia, in Belarus with my parents. But, like many parents that needed money, they sent me to America to live with my aunt Anna, never realizing that this was the start of my living nightmare.

Bertha Speaks from her grave about her memories.

THE BEGINNING

Clouds form.

A dark mist hangs over me.
The sun is gone, and smiles are hard to create.
Every day I wonder what hidden truth has yet to be revealed,
hidden deep down, buried, never to come to light.

I rarely smiled. I never had a happy childhood, and my parents were strict with us. Rules were followed, and smiles and hugs were few and far between. Growing up, I always felt alone and isolated. Extremely tall for my age, overweight yet pretty in my own way, I never expected what was about to happen, nor would I ever understand what I did to deserve what my parents did to me and being sent away.

My name is Bertha, and one morning when I entered the kitchen of my parents' home, a strange man was sitting at the kitchen table. Spread out on the table were papers, documents, and some legal papers that they were signing. They stopped talking when I entered the room, and went to get a cup of coffee and something from the fry pan to eat.

Sitting down next to my sister and my mother, I realized from their stares and the quiet that something was about to happen, and I did not understand or know what. The man sitting at the table—his name does not matter—told me to go into my room, pack my clothes in a small suitcase, and be ready to leave within the hour.

I hardly moved. My mother just bowed her head, and my father quickly grabbed me by the arms, shoving me into my room and demanding that I do what the man had said. Trying to ask why and what I had done did no good. When they finally did respond to my questions, they said I would find a better life in a new world, and that good things would happen to me. I would be blessed, and so would my family.

My sister, Bella, had sat at the table and

heard what my parents wanted for me. She hung her head because she wanted to be the one they sent, but for some reason, they wanted her to stay home. The man that had come told them they would still have Bella if I went to America. I begged them to send my sister, but they did not listen or care. Later, I would find out that she never made it out of Belarus, and I never saw her again. I never heard from my sister, and when living through what I am about to describe, I often thought of how she pleaded with my parents to send her to America.

I am not sure now just how many sisters and brothers I had, but from what I learned later, four came to the US. My sister never made it here to America. She was kept prisoner, you might say, in Belarus.

Leaving my home with nothing more than a suitcase filled with clothes, little money, and a strange man who was not mean yet not kind at all, I was taken to a boat called the New Amsterdam. My parents had paid for the passage on the boat, but the lies they told me about what my life and future held would haunt me forever. After being placed on it—all alone—I was told that I would be traveling to someplace called America, and that at the end of the journey someone would be there to meet me. The man left me in a room all alone with five other strange and scared young girls, saying he would find me when we were leaving the boat. I was about fourteen, and the year was 1913.

The trip took weeks and the waters were not always calm. Many of the passengers got sick. Cramped quarters, foul smells, and a lack of places to wash up—it was a miracle that I survived. The journey was long and hard. I got so sick I could hardly breathe at times from the close quarters, the lack of sunshine, and the hot air within the room. The windows in the cabin, I guess it was called, were darkened and we were not allowed on top of the boat to get air for more than one or two hours a day. The food was awful, but at least we had water. So, I boarded the New Amsterdam and arrived weeks later, sick, tired, gaunt, and dehydrated.

Ellis Island was where we were taken when the boat finally stopped. On arrival, I was interrogated and my papers checked. Arriving in America was a living nightmare after getting through the journey, meeting this man to enter Ellis Island, and then learning that I was going to live with an aunt and uncle that I did not know. I cried, and prayed that someone from my family would read my name on the paper I was holding up that said Bertha Birnbaum.

My family members arrived, but there was no hug or any warmth shown on their faces. An older woman grabbed my arm, dragged me into an old car, and took me to her home, where she gave me a corner of a piece of floor to clean, then placed a mat on a cot, with a thin blanket, there for me to sleep on. They worked me to death until I almost collapsed. I was to be their servant; after all, I lived in their home for free and needed to pay my way. I was terrified of this aunt, and just kept to myself and did what she asked. I cooked, cleaned, and served them day and night, and never received one kind word. It was a prison of a different kind.

Living there was worse than living on the boat for so many weeks. They demanded that I work as a seamstress in a factory, make all of their meals, and clean their clothes and their home as payment for living there. Most of my money was for my room and board, but some could be used for my own needs. I was always sad, and seldom smiled. My aunt Anna and her husband Milton were glad I was going to live with them—I would be their slave.

I met Morris at the factory where I was hired to sew. Daily, I was required to create over twenty-five dresses and ten shirts, or not get paid the ten cents a garment to bring money home to my aunt, who took most of it for herself and her family. Working in the factory was hard, but it got me out of the house and with other people. But no one really spoke while we worked, and lunch was at our machines for only fifteen short minutes. Bathroom breaks required someone walking us to the restroom and making sure that we returned within three minutes.

Life was hard, and the anger within me never left. I felt cheated, and I knew that my only way out was to find someone who would take my heart and care for me. Morris was that person. He saw something in me that no one else did, and we married. He thought I was beautiful, and would wine and dine me until I gave him four children.

Later, he thought me boring and needed some diversions of his own. He provided for us, but was gone many nights and would enter our bedroom in the early morning hours. At that time, I was caring for my two sons and my two daughters, and had little time to really reflect on my life and the fact that he cared for us, but in a lukewarm way. The passion had left after my fourth child was born.

Some say that I was sweet and a role model for my grandchildren, while others say I was bitter, angry, and never smiled. Both assessments are true. I hated my life with my aunt, and my children—Henry, David, Judy, and Lillian—were my life. But sometimes I was frustrated and needed to sound off, too. At times, I required that each of my children go to work and earn money to help pay bills that I needed paid. But when Morris died at an early age, I especially needed David, or Doc as he was called, to quit college and begin earning some money. He wanted to be a CPA, but instead earned about eighty dollars a week selling mattresses on the black market. I never questioned him, because he brought in the money. Later on, he was designated as 4F, but joined the merchant marines. Doc never graduated college and became a dry cleaner, but that's the breaks.

Life was hard after losing Morris, and at an older age when my four children were married, I made the mistake of marrying for convenience. I wound up with a man that my granddaughters felt was mean, abusive, and unfeeling. I once again became a maid, servant, chief cook, and bottle washer to Charlie, who was anything but warm. When we went to visit my children, he never smiled, never greeted them, and was always rude and distant. Too often, they just wanted him to leave.

My life became another nightmare living with Charlie, and things with my family deteriorated because he did not want them in my apartment, and would never let me visit them. However, I eventually learned how to use public transportation and managed to escape his clutches for short times, claiming that I needed to shop for food, extra milk, or other supplies like napkins or paper towels. In reality, one of my children met me a stop away, took me for lunch, and we tried to work out how I could leave him forever. He was terrible, cruel, and although he never used his hands on me, he was abusive in his words and actions. Marrying him placed me back in another prison, and when he got sick and had to go to the hospital, it was like a vacation from hell.

We were married for several years, and when he finally passed away, I was not sad but overjoyed. His children didn't even come to his funeral, nor were they ever a part of our miserable lives. Doc, my youngest, took care of everything, and had made sure at one point that Charlie knew his manners and that his ways and actions had better change toward me; for a time, they did. When I felt threatened again, I demanded that Doc take me to his sister's house, where I hoped to remain far away from this tyrant.

This lasted until he finally died, but my life was always hard. I began to resent what others had, which was a family filled with love and warmth. I guess I became hard myself, and when Lillian, Doc, Harold, and Judy all met in Lillian's house, the discussion got heated as to where I would remain and live. I did not want to go with anyone but George and my Lillian.

Life was hard for me, and if I could change anything, I would never have married Charlie, I would have tried harder with my grandchildren, and I might have even learned to smile. From the moment I set foot in America, I never had a day of love, happiness, or joy until I met Morris. But then the fire burned out like a candle with wax that slowly disappears, and so did my happiness forever.

Life gave me many ups and downs, but I never expected so many black aces and evil times to taint the love in my heart for so many that never would be revealed. When I moved in with my daughter, Lily, some of my grandchildren got to know the real Bertha, while others probably till this day would say, "She never smiled, laughed, or made us feel loved."

I had very little to smile about all my life. Some of my grandchildren brought me joy. They took care of me for my remaining years and made me smile, and I helped make their favorite dishes. Others I never gave a chance, and they will tell you till this day that I never smiled for them, never hugged them to show them any warmth, and for years to come my voice and thoughts remained silenced. I still don't smile.

KEEP SILENT: BESSIE THE TYRANT

How dare they complain that I want quiet in my classroom, and why would students dare to answer questions incorrectly? I can't stand wrong answers, and those that dare to give them get the wrath of this person big time.

Sitting in their seats in their neat rows, staring at me while I sit at my desk, dishing out assignments and expecting quiet and compliance the entire day, someone dared to ask me a question about one of the math problems. You moron, you idiot! How dare you question me? You should know this work from last year, and if you don't, figure it out. It's not my job to tell you the answers. And when the time comes to go over them, you'd better keep silent and listen to the responses of those that are smart—not like you. My job is not to teach anything, and not to be disturbed while writing my memoirs and dealing with becoming a published author. Your job is to shut up and stay silent, and don't make me angry or you will feel pain in more ways than one.

Ferndine would not allow the other student to shut up and answered for her. "How are we supposed to learn and do the problems if we never saw this before?"

Just as she was about to ask more, Rosen slammed her fist in Ferndine's face and dared her to tell anyone how she got the mark on her cheek. But Ferndine would not stop and the other students cowered, sliding down in their seats and praying that they would not be next—or worse.   One of the boys got up and dared to walk over to Rosen. Rosen took her large ruler and slammed him in the leg. Poor Marcus would not be able to play on the baseball team for a long time. She literally injured his leg so badly he could barely walk, and when he told his parents later in the day, they told him he was wrong for disrespecting the teacher.

I rule this room, and how dare anyone defy me? Just for what Ferndine and Marcus did I gave the whole class an assignment to define a hundred words, compose sentences, and write a composition about why they should not question the teacher—ever! No one said a word as I told them to open their books to the math problems they were working on, and now we would go over the answers. Surely they didn't think I was going to show them how to do them. Why should I? They were old enough to use their computers to find examples of these problems, and then get the right answers.

Going around the room starting with problem one, I made each student give their response until we completed all fifty problems. Anyone who gave the wrong answers got their hands slapped with the ruler. This became time consuming and tiresome. Only one student, Pamela, knew anything, and she insisted on giving all the responses so that I would not be upset anymore. Nor did she care if I gave a huge punishment to the rest of the class for homework. Which I did!

Things were done for the day, and the class was told to dismiss themselves since I hated walking down the steps with them because they would probably push me. And then where would they be without this great teacher?

The students filed out of the yard and Ferndine ran over to her mother, who was the PTA president of the school, and told her what had happened. Going to the superintendent was a joke since he was my brother. Going to the police chief, my uncle, would not work either! Ferndine decided to take her own action, thinking that going to the news would break open a story and make them look into my methods. How dare she think she would get away with this?

Ferndine thought she could take me out. She was just a wimpy kid in the sixth grade who hid behind her aunt in the next classroom, or her mother, who was the PTA president of the school and thought that her precious child was so amazing, smart, and wonderful. That might be the case, but I thought not! She was just a plain and ordinary kid who might be smart, but not smart enough to outsmart what I had in store for her and some of the others in the class.

The fire department of New York was holding a contest for the best compositions dealing with fire prevention. Of course, someone just might win for the school, but I was the greatest teacher and wanted to be sure that one of my students won for the district, and hopefully the city. Students were to write their stories or compositions in class with access to information given to us by the fire department, making sure what they wrote was accurate but written in their own words. They needed to include why fire prevention knowledge was vital and important, and use other research that might help the public understand what to do when and if a fire broke out in their homes.

Each student worked on his/her composition for over a week, and then the big reveal came. Each composition was numbered, and no names were on any of them so that when the panel of judges, namely the fourth and fifth grade teachers, the reading teacher, and the writing teacher, judged them, no one knew whose classes they came from.

The principal called in all the grade six teachers and announced the winners. Would you dare to believe that Ferndine's was the best one, and my Pamela came in tenth? How dare they choose her?

***

I had always excelled in school, but for some reason, this teacher resented me because of my mother and my aunt. I was not the prettiest girl in the world—I was overweight and awkward at times—but had some friends in this class. Yet Bessie hated me because I was smart, and because my aunt happened to be a better educator than Bessie would ever be. I was never rude or disrespectful, but sometimes it's hard to hold your tongue.

***

I decided to make sure that Ferndine did not win by saying that her aunt, who taught grade six, might have told her what to write, even though Ferndine wrote it in class and learned about it at the same time as everyone else. Or did she?

The principal did not want to disqualify her, but I finally convinced them to take another look at Pamela's and Jeffrey's compositions, and both were chosen to send to the fire department and the district. I then announced the winners to the class, and made sure that Ferndine knew that I knew she'd had help.

Well, never in all my years had any student dared to talk back to me, or even doubt my words. She exploded, and told me that I had no right to accuse her of cheating. I had no right to disqualify her composition, which would probably have won for the district and maybe the city. She said, "You are the poorest excuse for something, but you're not an educator. All you ever do is criticize me because my aunt teaches here, and you can't hold a candle to her. Yours is all burnt out! How dare you say that I cheated, and how dare you embarrass me, you OLD WITCH, in front of this class? I'm going to the office and voicing my thoughts. I won't be silenced this time."

Ferndine did go to the principal's office, and he did agree with her, but that was too bad. The class felt she did deserve to win, but I won this one since my brother was the superintendent of the district and he backed me up big time. Ferndine took several days off because she was upset. Too bad. I could not understand the big deal; it was just a contest. But I guess since she might never see any other wins in her life, this one was too bad.

Ferndine reported my actions and what I had said, but since I was protected, she lost her battle and someone else won the contest. No one in this school was awarded the first prize from the city, but my brother made sure that my precious Pamela got first prize for the district, making me come out on top.

The rest of the year was not very much different. The science fair was the last major event, and I paired Ferndine with someone she did not really like. But who cared? She was not going to get a perfect grade no matter what. She had dared to defy me, and now I held all the cards—or so I thought. But someone decided to take matters in a different direction.

Walking into the classroom the next morning and unlocking the doors, putting my coat in my own private closet, I saw that someone had left me a message on the mirror—an X in red, which could have been blood or paint—and my picture underneath it. The caption said: Watch your back!

Shaking and scared, I thought it was just a stupid prank. But who would be able to open the padlock on my closet and put that message there? The custodian and the principal came up and I asked that they call the police, but they refused. They said to just ignore it, and they would try and find out who was behind the prank. But whoever this was, they were just getting started.

The class came in, and of course I was not in the mood for anything they would say or do, so I give them a hundred words to define and dared anyone to speak or not work. At lunchtime, I took them to the lunchroom, but not before locking my closet with the new padlock the custodian had put on the door, locking my classroom with the new keys, and then heading down to eat my lunch with other staff members, who'd heard about the incident. No one said anything.

When I went back to my classroom to retrieve my coat to pick up my students in the outer yard, the door was filled with red blood or paint, skeletons hung from the door with my face on all of them, and a note said, Change your ways before it's too late! Was this a threat, or was someone telling me I was an awful person?

This really had me thinking it was either another teacher or a student. We did not have cameras in the halls or in the classrooms, and no one had seen anyone near my door, since the floor was empty of staff and students at the time due to an emergency fire drill that came out of nowhere. Someone pulled the fire alarm just as I was going down to pick up the class even though I had no coat, because I did not want to touch the door, hoping they would get prints from the message or somewhere on the door. Thankfully, it was fifty degrees, but still we were cold, and were out there for a while.

When we were permitted to reenter, I did not want my students to see the door, but I was told that there was nothing on it to see.

Someone had cleaned the door, and everyone thought I'd imagined it all. They even said there was nothing on the mirror in my closet, even though the custodian had seen it. He made it sound like I'd made it up. Was someone gaslighting me?

I refused to let this get to me until I realized that something was really wrong the next day. I entered my classroom and the desks were all turned over, the books were thrown around the room, and my desk was covered with real blood—at least it looked like it. Someone had placed a mask on the desk with my face on it, with cuts, scratches, and slits, letting me know that they were watching my every move. For the first time in my life, I was afraid, and I thought about running out of the school and never coming back. My classroom was in total disarray, and I went down to the office to report it. But when they came up with me to my classroom, everything was just the way I'd left it the day before. They said I must have seen a hallucination, and they thought I was losing my mind.

Deciding to leave for the day, I went to my car, which I thought was parked in the lot next to the school. It was gone! How? I called for help using my phone, but no one came. The battery was dead, and it appeared it might not have been booted up correctly. But then someone called, and the voice on the other end of the phone laughed heinously.

The next thing I knew I was in a hospital room, my hands restrained, and I could not move. A stark looking nurse in a uniform entered with a syringe in her hand. She said she was going to put whatever was in the syringe into the IV, thus into me. I could hardly speak, and I was terrified. She said she was going to give me something to calm me down, that I had been out of control, screaming, hitting, yelling, and claiming someone was out to kill me. Everyone in the school said that what I thought I saw never happened. No one believed anything I said.

For the next ten years, I lived in hell in that place, with treatments, psych evaluations, no visitors, and in isolation. When I finally could enter the room with some other residents, I was told to confine myself to a simple chair, watch television, and not speak to anyone. They were afraid I would get violent.

I hardly remember anything that happened before, and now that I am no longer there and was put to rest in this place, my voice has been silenced, too. Does anyone care?

HER FINAL REPOSE

Hidden beneath a stone with my eyes wide open and my body covered in a sheet, nothing below the sheet. I was buried alive to live out my final hours in this airtight coffin. Just why this happened to me, and how, will be revealed slowly and methodically. I hope someone will dig deep into the ground, hear my screams, and save me before the bugs eat their way through my thin sheet, destroy my face, and take away my last ounce of breath.

My hands have been tied to the side of the coffin in such a way that I cannot move them. My legs are bound and my mouth was taped, but I managed to get it off somehow. Life handed me a tough deal, and my final repose is where I wound up. I'll tell you my story, and you can decide if I belong in the ground and behind this next stone that is unmarked.

My name is Benita, and I was once a prostitute, pole dancer, and soap star who managed to get along with the help of the johns that I screwed; the men that gave me money that I allowed them to stick where ever they wanted, and who showed me a good time—I showed them even more. Some were married. The director of the soap that I starred in used me for his own pleasures in order to keep me employed. If not, I would have been fired. You see, I am not a great actress, but am a fantastic bed partner.

When I realized that I needed more than what I was doing, I decided to take on another role which would require some acting skills on my part. But I thought that I could handle pretending that I knew how to handle the daily events needed to run a catering hall and the employees. The catering hall was in a small town, and the owner took to my appearance in a heartbeat. Alonzo Rivera was his name, and his wife ran the office. She had dark hair in a bun, thick glasses, was overweight, and had a hardcore attitude and personality. When Alonzo hired me, she was not at all happy.

Starting my job and learning my duties, I realized that I would help plan weddings, parties, retirement parties, business meetings, and other events. My job would be to make sure that there were not more than three events daily. No one watched over what I was doing, and each type of event had its own planning sheet, prices, and costs. No one would notice if I added some zeros to some of the smaller items—the cost of flowers, music, and even invitations and place cards—always handing in the right invoices and giving the customer the other. I always requested that they give me cash for these incidentals so that they would not be taxed. No one ever questioned me; at least not until Sarah Jones came into my life and the nightmare began.

Sarah Jones was a rich bitch who had

more money than she needed. So what if I fleeced her out of some? Sarah came from a rich family, but she had made it on her own. She was a criminal defense lawyer, and was married to a doctor who had several offices all over the state. Her two sisters were not quite as well off, but she couldn't care less about them. I found out their finances were not quite as lucrative as hers, and they were always asking her for help, but she ignored them. I found this out by prying into her life and asking questions, just to pretend to get to know her better. She felt that she worked for what she had, and so should they.

Sarah entered my office wearing a black pencil-thin, straight skirt, a white turtle neck, and a black jacket buttoned in the center. Her five-inch heels came from *Nordstrom*, and her handbag was from *Kate Spade*. She oozed money, and her personality oozed "Don't dare go against my wishes." Her handshake was strong and her grip even stronger, and she did not smile or show any emotions.

Requesting to see the various packages for the events that she wanted to host, I showed her those for business meetings with lunch, breakfast meetings, and late-night parties with cocktails, drinks, and music. Looking them over, I then explained that certain incidentals needed to be paid for in cash in order to lower the taxes and give her a ten percent discount on all the packages. She seemed suspect at first but finally agreed, but insisted on a written statement of all her costs, including those that she paid for in cash. Hesitating, I told her that it would create a problem but, in the end, I had no choice. Rather than lose the money or fear that she would tell my boss what I was doing, I decided to add some extras to the parties on us, and then created another invoice with the incidentals but jacking up the prices in order that I profited some more.

Signing the forms and leaving a deposit for the three events—the luncheon, the breakfast, and the night time event—she took home the sheet with what was included for each one, and then would let me know if there was anything else she needed besides staff to run each event. She wanted to interview each one before agreeing to finalize the plans.

Sarah returned to the catering hall and was met by Alonzo and his wife Carmella, who from the start had hated me and wanted me out of the way. I never realized that she was the brains behind the business, and that Sarah had her in her hip pocket all the time. Sarah Jones might have billed herself as a lawyer, but she was an undercover agent for the FBI and worked part time for the US Treasury, taking on cases where money laundering was involved, finances were in question, and, in my case, mishandling of payments for the events had occurred.

But that was not all. Someone coming to book a party thought they recognized me from somewhere else and called me by another name. I felt like my face turned as pale as a ghost and I began to shake, not knowing which way to turn. My flesh seemed clammy and my body ice cold. Sarah knew something about me, but she had not revealed anything, nor had she made any attempt to let me know that she was aware of my past. Signing the forms for all the events, I felt that I had to get out really fast—I felt sick, and hoped to escape and find myself somewhere else. The need to move and leave this lucrative job might be necessary.

But just as I was about to open the door and exit, Sarah stood in my way, along with several others who seemed to be law enforcement. I would learn their true calling soon enough.

They handcuffed me, put me in the back of a tinted windowed car, and made sure that I was flanked on all sides so that I could not move or attempt to get out, letting me know that there was no escape this time and that I would pay for all that I had done. I had no idea what she'd found out or who these people were, but I realized that someone within the catering business, namely the wife, had decided it was time to end my reign, keep me away from Alonzo, and make sure that I would disappear. Was she connected to the mob? Was she aware of who I was connected to? Or was I used as a pawn all the time just to get even for something I did as a teen?

Growing up, I'd had nothing, and my mother left me alone at night to have some fun with her boyfriends. My father worked three jobs to keep a roof over our heads. My mother always seemed to have money, buying herself expensive clothes and shoes, and I wore the same dresses and shoes for years, never seeing anything new unless it was for my birthday.

There comes a time when you must decide, and for me, it came when I was eighteen and realized that I needed to take control of my destiny, even if it meant eliminating certain people and benefitting from their demise. Little did I know that someone I would meet in the present had seen what I did in the past. Little did I know that I had an aunt named Rosita, and that she had a daughter named Sarah Jones from her second husband, and that Sarah saw what I did but never told on me until now.

Sarah was just a child when it happened, and her mother told her she'd imagined what she saw. Then, after seeing proof, she said to keep it quiet or they might be next. "Benita is dangerous. You saw what she did to her poor mother. If she knows that you saw her cut her up, sticking a knife into her heart and then taking apart the body and putting it in a plastic bag, then throwing each piece in many different places, we could be next." What I did not know was that fourteen-year-old Sarah had a phone in her hand and videotaped the entire event, hoping to show it to the police. Recording it was just the beginning, and facing her now in the present would end it all. Or would it?

My body confined to the car, my thoughts were trying to figure a way out of my situation. But at the end or the journey, I was at the cemetery. The gravediggers had already dug my final resting place, where I would spend eternity. But not until Sarah had her moment. A few people were with her, and Sarah showed them her videos of what I'd done to my mother, my affairs, the money they knew I'd stolen, and more, taking away the lives of so many.

I was taken from the car, placed in the coffin with just a sheet over me and a small pillow for my head, my hands bound across my chest and my eyes opened wide. My legs were bound, and they tossed me in and closed the lid, sealing it until the very end.

I am behind the next stone that has moss covering it, in brown and decaying grounds that have not been cared for in years. This cemetery is old, and those buried here are long forgotten for the deeds that they inflicted on others.

My eyes are starting to close as I begin to feel some bugs within them, and I am trying to blink them out but cannot. My head feels heavy as the bugs have started crawling around on my face. I have been down here for several days. I've managed to stay alive because, even though my hands are bound, I am able to drink the water they left for me for one week, because of the way they have been placed. However, one of the restraints came out, and now I can untie the other. My legs are free, but the lid on the coffin has been nailed shut, and I am buried ten feet below the ground. No one out there can hear my cries.

The air is beginning to turn black all around me, and I am feeling the darkness within my body and soul. The graveyard is quiet, but even though I am ten feet below the ground I feel that someone is watching me.

I hear a shrill cry above me. Is it

another victim being placed in this solitary cemetery for those that have wronged others? There are not ghosts here but something is happening, and I hear something above me. Oh my god. It's a bulldozer, and they are about to level the cemetery—anyone buried will be crushed in the process. I start to hear drilling and banging. It's hard fighting the urge to cry, and I know it's a matter of minutes before I will feel the heat as the flames engulf what is left of the coffins. I heard they will burn them all, leaving no evidence that anyone has even been buried here. It will be like I never existed.

The drilling and banging continue until I feel a chill of cold air on my face, as the lid of the coffin is now open. Staring down at me is a face that I will never forget, one that will haunt me in eternity forever. The face staring down at me is that of the one person that I thought was dead, mutilated, and buried.

Whose face?

"I wanted my face to be the last one that you ever saw before this lid is permanently closed, your body sealed within this coffin forever, then your last breath finally taken. Remember my smile. Remember my face. Rot in hell!

"Your voice will be more than silenced, and your ability to even communicate will be taken."

Someone lowers themselves into my coffin, opens my mouth, and rips out my tongue and voice box, and I slowly close my eyes for the last time, no longer with any hint of a smile. My voice is silenced forever.

THE GRANDMOTHER

All my life I had to struggle and work hard for everything that I ever needed. So, why not take advantage of a situation? My grandmother, Gertie, was frail and much older, needing constant care at home. Her mind was sharp, but her legs were weak. She could no longer shop for herself, and going to the bank to deposit her disability checks had become a real chore. Each one of us had a different father, and not one of us had all of the conveniences that life should have given us. So, we joined forces to get what we deserved from our grandmother. Doreen was a maid, Janet worked in a bar, and Eileen collected unemployment checks every time she was fired from her job. She had worked as a waitress, receptionist, and barrister, but had difficulty getting along with women. So, naturally, when she had to serve them or deal with their appointments, needless to say, she came up short.

My sisters and I had decided to take on the responsibility of her daily care. Of course, I felt, as they did, that we deserved something for our efforts. Moving into her huge house was not a problem, as she had six bedrooms, three baths, and enough closet space for everyone. The house was amazing and the kitchen was state of the art. Taking some of what she had was not a problem until she began to realize that something was wrong.

In order to pay her bills, take her to doctors, and deal with the transportation, get her medication, and anything else she needed, I told her we needed access to her bank accounts, ATM cards and passwords, and anything else that would help each one of us take care of her daily financial expenses. The house was paid for, but she still had electricity and phone bills, and other incidental expenses.

But she was sharp and would not let

anyone reconcile her checkbook, thinking that we would never rip her off but not really knowing for sure. She asked for receipts for food, medication, and anything that we needed to get for her, but she never realized, thank heaven, that we used her ATM card to get cash and then deposited it into each of our own accounts or wallets. For some reason, every one of her charge cards allowed cash advances, and we were all careful not to go over the limit or close to it. When the bills came, we told her we'd pay them from her checkbooks so that she would not realize that we were taking money out via the cash advances.

For the first few weeks, everything went according to plan, until I found her will and her bequests. Everything she had—and it was millions in stocks, IRAs, funds in her accounts, her house, her bank accounts, personal possessions—she was leaving to different charities. She was married to my grandfather and they never had children of their own. She was his second wife. My real grandmother, Fanny, died from pneumonia and she married him. He left it all to her, and she left it all to charities. Her way of her of giving back to others who were less fortunate.

But, what about us? My two sisters and I decided to do something about it and went to a lawyer, hoping to declare her incompetent and not able to make any rational decisions on her own. Her medication regimen was spelled out and we gave it to her, but adding some extra to her coffee was not noticed. Adding more crushed up blood pressure medication to her oatmeal was never noticed at any time. She became disoriented at times when we decided to add other medications to her juice, since some were clear liquids and others were not.

When we invited the lawyer to come to her home, he saw that she was declining and needed someone to take over power of attorney. At times, she was lucid, but at others, simply out of it. Since my sister was an expert forger, we were able to add some addendums to the will, stating that she wanted each one of us to have something for taking care of her in her final months or days.

I wanted the house. Doreen, my older sister, wanted her car and her stocks. I wanted the IRAs, and my younger sister, Eileen, her clothes, shoes, and some money. We found a notary that notarized the new copy and it looked quite authentic, but would the lawyer notice the changes, and did he have a copy of the original one? We thought fast, and when he noticed that it was dated after the original one, I stated that I had another lawyer draw it up and had it notarized. Not sure whether to believe us or not, he wanted the name of the other lawyer, at which time we had to put Plan B into action and take care of this person before our entire plan was ruined.

***

They thought they were so clever and that I didn't know what they were planning and had been doing. This is Gertie, and I was quite aware of what my so-called "caring" granddaughters had planned for my sudden and lucrative demise. There were cameras all over the house, hidden in corners that they would never notice. I had my phones bugged so that I could listen in on conversations at any time. My cell phone was hidden away, and no one even knew that I had one. Inside the back closet in my room I had a refrigerator that stored anything that I needed to keep cold, and I had been storing away whatever they made for me to prove that I was being over medicated, and, even worse, poisoned by my own granddaughters. They would leave the trays, and I emptied all of the contents into containers, stored them in this refrigerator, labelled them with what they were supposed to contain—and, of course, the medications and other pills that had been added—and then stored them away and made a phone call to a friend in law enforcement, asking what to do next in order to take them all down. I had the proof, but I needed to get them to admit that they forged my signature on documents, that the lawyer they claimed wrote the new will was their cousin Todd and that it was bogus, and then the tables would be turned. SOON!

Everyone was convinced that I had a touch of dementia. I had them all fooled. Sure, it was easy to forget where I put my glasses or which pair of shoes to wear. I could easily forget where I put my favorite mug, or my address, or how to add simple numbers, but I was sharp as a tack. Fortunately, my acting lessons as an adult in the small theater company were coming in handy.

Janet was about to enter my room, carrying what looked like a dish of vanilla ice cream with something on top. Who knew what pills she'd crushed? And she thought I didn't know she was using food coloring to camouflage her deceptions.

Janet had a peanut allergy. Eileen was a diabetic, and the other sister, Doreen, was allergic to milk protein and shellfish. What a pity that I knew this, because this information would help me take care of all three of them at the dinner party that I had planned the following Saturday night.

Planning the meal would not be that easy, but using the proper ingredients to take care of all three of them would not be hard. Grilled chicken cooked in peanut oil; how simple was that? Nuts ground into a fine powder would not be detected, and Janet would never suspect. Using my powdered sugar, I could create delicious muffins and donuts, and tell everyone that they were sugar-free, pretending to have bought them in a bakery that sold sugar free baked goods and cookies, using an old bakery box that I had stored away. Scallops, and, of course, shrimp, were deadly to Doreen, but she'd never know they were in the soup, as I shredded them so finely that she'd never even realize it until it was too late. Doreen was allergic to shrimp, and what a pity that she wouldn't see it coming.

Eileen was a diabetic. Taking care of her would not be hard, as she would think the dessert was sugar free and made with no sugar at all. But I packed it in, and by the time she ate several pieces of pastry, her sugar level should rise, I hoped, just enough.

The party was going to begin at eight promptly, with the servers bringing everyone their special cocktails. The three girls were there, and I had also invited several older friends that were still around. The meal would be a sit down, and each place card on the table would direct the guests as to where to sit, hoping they would have great companions on either side of them.

The first dish was a salad; everyone was safe with that. Then orders would be taken for soups, entrees, and desserts as the main event was about to begin. Each course was planned by me, Gertie, and although they still think I am senile or have dementia, I hope the last food laugh will be mine.

The first course would be soup, and this was where things might get interesting, as I had made sure that within the soup was not only chicken stock, but shrimp stock. Checking out the guests, everyone seemed to be enjoying it since I had made sure that there were pieces of celery, carrots, and, of course, chicken in the broth that was also made of shrimp stock.

Knowing my guests, I knew that only Doreen was allergic to shrimp, but I made sure that her first dish was chicken—I did not want the fun to start too early. Next, Janet ordered grilled chicken. The first piece was grilled in olive oil, but the second would be cooked in peanut oil. Finally, the dessert would be the best yet, as I had laced it with different kinds of sugar so that anyone sitting there would have a sugar rush—especially Eileen.

Now the fun began, as the next course was about to be served. The grilled chicken was up first. Watching as Janet devoured the first piece and started on the second, I could see that she was having a reaction. There was no epinephrine auto-injector to stop the attack. She had one, but it had mysteriously disappeared. She said that her eyes were bothering her, her throat was closing, and she felt awful, so I offered her some water and told her maybe she'd eaten too fast. Her nose started to run, and she began to feel itching and tingling in and around her mouth and throat. She could barely talk. One of my guests was a doctor, and thought maybe she had eaten something that went down the wrong way. Then he realized she was having a seizure, never thinking it was an allergy. So, they called 911 and took her to the ER, where they would sort it out.

But, since this group was not really concerned about Janet or what was wrong—even her sisters did not stop to comfort her—

the next course would be the shrimp, and I hoped that Doreen did not react too fast. Thinking about it, I decided to hold off on this one, because it might look suspicious. Next, of course, was dessert, and that would take care of Eileen—maybe not right away, but within the next day or more.

Doreen was disappointed in the cod fish, but I wanted to make sure that no one else had any reactions to the food or they would suspect me. But, of course, I would blame it on the chef.

The hospital called and said that Janet did not make it, and that she'd had some kind or reaction to the food, but they had no idea what it was. I made sure that all the chicken that was left over was gone, and that her plate was broken into pieces and destroyed, never to be recovered. The spoons, knives, and other utensils were destroyed as well, so hopefully they would not figure it out.

Funeral arrangements would have to wait for a while, as poor Eileen checked her sugar levels and needed to go to the ER, too. I pretended not to understand how the bakery would dare to send anything but sugar free pastries and cookies. I told everyone that I had not ordered anything other than diabetic desserts. And I was so saddened to learn that Eileen had not even made it to the ER.

The next day, Doreen went to the freezer and pulled out what she thought was cod or catfish. She just pulled it out of the freezer and then proceeded to fry it up the way she liked it. She never realized that it was shrimp, because I had taken off the tails, cut them in small pieces, and deveined them, hoping she would not know what they were. She even prepared a salad and some pasta.

Starting to eat them, she felt fine, but within a few minutes, her mouth tingled, she was nauseous, had itching skin, and her throat was closing. So sad that no one was there to help her, and her throat was so tight that when she called 911 and gave her location, that's all she could say. They took her to the ER and tried their best, but poor Doreen did not make it. I never knew she was also allergic to peanut oil, which she'd used instead of the olive oil since I put the peanut oil in the olive oil bottle.

Three down and all gone. What a pity!

Before each one of them went to the ER, I gave them my special smile, letting them know that I felt so sad for what had happened to them. Called to the hospital to say goodbye to each one of my granddaughters in private, I imparted on all three, since they were in the same place, that they never should have underestimated me, or thought that I didn't know what they were planning. Now they are finally three more voices that are silenced.

THE CON ARTISTS

The darkness envelopes the next three bodies that are hidden behind stones quite different from the ones in many cemeteries. The surrounding area is desolate, and there are never any visitors here. On each stone is the face of the person beneath the stone as they appeared at their death. Whether they were murdered, beaten, or tortured, their final expressions were photographed and their faces engraved on each stone, with their exact final expressions of terror. This is a cemetery that no one dares to enter, as some think those beneath the stones rise at night. Each one of these evil coffin dwellers did something so heinous, so horrendous, that their final fates belong in this cemetery called the Gravediggers Delight.

A judge will tell the story of these three grave dwellers, who are here because they did something to other people that warranted being placed in this horrific place. Their tortured souls and bodies will rot within the confines of their coffins, which are just wooden boxes nailed shut. Their final repose and their burial were nothing more than the gravediggers digging holes and literally dropping the coffins in them, and then covering them with sand.

My name is Judge Stanford Brown, and I am your narrator. For most of my life I practiced law, until I was finally appointed to the bench. However, marrying my wife, Denise, I learned that her father was connected to the mob and was a higher up drug lord, which I did not know when I signed the prenup before marrying someone half my age. Learning the ropes about being his son-in-law, it became apparent that when members of his drug team or members of his family came into my court, I had better make sure that they did not get jail time and that bail was set.

Marvin was my accountant, and he dealt with my taxes, books, and more. He was relatively honest until he was not. You'll hear more about this as the story unfolds.

Daniel was the final member of this group. He was our lawyer, and if you think dishonest wait until you learn more about him.

This is their story: The Judge, the Lawyer, and the Accountant.

***

This cemetery has us backed away in three wooden coffins, nailed shut. I can imagine you are wondering just why we are being treated as if we are undesirables, untouchables, and horrific souls that will be haunted for all eternity. What could each of us have done?

Morris was the accountant for my law firm, and he managed to help me fudge the books so that my partners never knew why we were always in the red. My accounts were in the black, but in foreign banks under an alias. John, the judge, knew of our dealings, since Morris was his lawyer, too, for other enterprises that he was into. For example, when some top mob bosses came up for trial and were sent to his courtroom, for some reason, they never got any real prison time, and some got off with a fine. John was connected to these people and took bribes, mostly because if he did not pass the right sentence, they would take down his family and some of his friends, teaching him a lesson to never cross the mob bosses.

The mob boss's son was a captain in the local police force, and his uncle was the chief of police. Possession of drugs, guns, and other small weapons, money laundering, mob kills that would appear to be accidents, and other crimes were just a few that no one could or would be able to prove.

No one ever really knew about our connection until a reporter named Stella overheard something that would take us all down. Just why she was still walking around was beyond all of us, and just how she managed to infiltrate our group is what I will relate next.

Stella was a double agent who appeared to be a reporter, but she was the daughter of the mob boss, and managed to overhear us talking about trying to disconnect ourselves from the mob and attempt to run a legitimate business. Well, not quite legit, but no longer having to pay them protection money, take bribes to fix cases, and, of course, do the once in a while odd jobs that they required in order for us to stay afloat.

***

This is John, the judge. Stella came to my courtroom pretending to cover the story of Antonio, accused of killing the butcher on our street. Of course, he claimed it was not him but someone else, but the cameras in the store showed that it was him. Somehow, when the evidence was to be presented in court by the prosecutor, the tapes disappeared from the evidence room, the notes prepared by the arresting detective were not placed in evidence, and the arresting officer went missing.

What happened next was not expected, and the result was that the prosecuting attorney and the defense attorney had to decide whether to proceed with the case or set Antonio free, knowing that he did kill the butcher. Could this somehow be connected to someone on the force? Was there someone that owed Antonio a favor?

Somehow, this required a decision from me, the judge, and I realized that it would place me in an odd position if I let Antonio go. But I had to come up with a way to create some doubt in the jury's mind that this man was guilty.

Lying and cover-ups were becoming the norm in my courtroom. My connection to Antonio and his family was not known. My grandson was married to his granddaughter, making it hard for me to bring the hammer down on him. Antonio was one of the tops in this mob family, involved in murder, money laundering, drug dealing, and funneling weapons of all kinds through different channels to arms dealers throughout the world, and even to young kids on the street who wanted to make a buck selling for them.

Taking my gavel in my hand, I stated that I would allow forty-eight hours for both sides to try and get to the bottom of the missing evidence, and possibly find the missing arresting officer. Did I know where the officer was? Did I know where the evidence went?

Someone decided that they would take all of us down. Stella was dangerous, posing as a reporter for a newspaper but connected to the mob, and after overhearing our conversations, she reported back to the mob head. That's when things began to fall apart.

One of the jury members got sick, or at least said she was ill with stomach pains, and then collapsed in the courtroom, causing us to stop everything and call 911. She had been planted there to divert everyone's attention, pretending to be sick after purposely eating something she knew would irritate her stomach. Spice gave her heartburn, and she purposely did not take her *Nexium*. Her chest pains appeared to be real, and her heartburn was over the top, she said. But was she that much in pain? I doubted it, but she accomplished what needed to be done. I had made sure she was on the jury, and that stopped the proceedings so that I could get a handle on what I had to do next.

Court had to be adjourned until we knew what happened to this juror, and an alternate was not in the cards if I wanted the trial to turn out the right way. Hoping that no one else got sick for legitimate reasons, we adjourned for the day, and court would reconvene in the morning at nine promptly.

Things do not always turn out the way you want. Something was wrong with this juror that even she did not know, and the result was she would not be returning any time soon. Now what was I going to do? After all, she was the foreman, and would have been able to sway the jury either to acquit the defendant or to consider a hung jury.

Both attorneys wanted this over with, but no one more than me, so I came up with an idea that I hoped would not backfire. With an alternate juror in place who seemed attracted to me, I insisted on questioning her in my chambers. What transpired I hoped would lead the verdict in the direction that I hoped for.

But something strange happened when I went back on the bench. My coffee cup was on my desk. I got up for ten seconds to use the bathroom to wash my hands, and never thought that anyone would taint my coffee with something that would take me out of commission for good. As the jury was now in place and the trial resumed, I felt pains in my stomach, hot flashes, and then keeled over. The next thing I knew I was being placed on a stretcher, and the EMT looked me straight in the eye and said this was a present from Antonio.

This might be the end of my story, but I am sure there are others that will suffer at the hand of this man because of what he wanted hidden. My voice is silenced; let's hope more will be, too!

LIES

This stone is devoted to me because I broke some serious laws, and wound up with a death sentence because I dared to not lie but tell the truth. Lies are what this country, that I was born in, was founded and made on. Telling the truth, the whole truth can often hurt someone's feelings, and make them worry when it's not needed. Telling someone they look ugly or need to go on a diet, even if you're just trying to be honest, is the wrong way to go where I come from. But if someone has a fatal illness, is it better to sugarcoat it and not come clean with the entire truth by telling them they have only a few months to live?

The truth is supposed to set you free, but in this case it would not. My name is Don, and all of my life I tried to always be honest, truthful, and never tell a lie. But the state that I live in as an adult passed a law stating that being too truthful was sinful, and that being brutally honest and telling the truth was punishable. Your sentence would depend on how strong that truth was or how many you told. This is what was decided.

When asked a question, we must think hard before giving a response, as there are people all around that will know that we told the truth since we all wear these truth detectors that are part of our everyday wardrobes. Small little wrist bands that have chips and special sensors help the police or anyone you are near know when you have strayed from telling a lie.

Children are great at lying, and love the fact that when they fail all of their subjects in school they can tell their parents they passed with all As or Bs. They bury the real report card and create one on their computers, print it out—since they all have the templates for the cards—and then show their parents how bright and wonderful they are. But some parents dare to question their children when they don't graduate on time. These inventive liars come up with the fact if they stay one more year, they get college credit and can get into any school with courses under their belt. Of course, their parents believe them, and would never dare think or say the truth: YOU LIED!

Today started out as any day at work. I work for doctors as a medical assistant, and can do X-rays. To save money, they even sent me to school to learn how to read the X-rays, so they do not need to send them to another radiologist to be read. But remember, lies are the foundation of our world, and telling a patient the truth about their condition is illegal. It works both ways. However, that's not what got me in trouble.

When things started to quiet down at work and I investigated some old cases where a diagnosis was given—and of course it was a total lie—I began wondering just how many people had died because of me, and because the doctors did not tell them the truth about their conditions. Lives were at stake, but it was thought better not to upset people. So what if they think they are healthy! Who cares?! In reality, something within me felt a certain tinge of guilt, but since it was a law and I knew that somehow they would find out if I dared to tell the truth, I fudged my statements and made people feel better about themselves or their illnesses.

Sidney was a man of means, and age sixty-five when he came to Dr. N's office for his annual checkup. The usual blood tests were taken, a general exam done, but when the doctor checked his blood pressure, it was off the charts. The patient saw that it said 173/90, but the doctor told him he was having trouble with the blood pressure machine and not to worry about what it registered. Sidney was overweight and breathing with difficulty, but the doctor discounted that, too, stating that he might just be nervous. Sending him for a chest X-ray and a cat scan, the doctor could see signs of clots in his lungs, blockages, and other indications that he might need further tests, and should have been referred to a heart doctor for a follow up. But instead, Dr. N told him to go on a diet, lose weight, walk or join a gym, and not to worry about anything, that his tests had come back with no anomalies, nothing that stuck out as unusual, and said, "See you next year."

I began feeling more pangs of guilt, but could not say anything as the doctor was in charge. When Sidney asked for a written report of his test results, I knew that this was my chance to help him even if it meant telling the truth. However, the doctor read over the report that I prepared, and I knew that I'd missed my chance since he had to sign off on it.

Lying is okay if it does not hurt anyone or hinder their lives. Telling a child that they play the piano well even if they do not is not that bad, since we hope it won't hurt their feelings or discourage them from trying harder. Lying is okay when you tell a child that he/she will become a singing star and you know he/she is tone deaf. But the child is only five, so no big deal. Lying is fine when you go into a bank and claim you need a loan because you want to buy a new house for your family, but you want the money for something else. Lying is okay when you can justify the reasons and can live with yourself after you tell the lies: You look amazing. (When the person looks like a fat cow); that dress looks great on you, Mrs. Jones. (It's two sizes too small, but she is smiling as she buys five more and you get the big sale). What about the car salesman that sells you a used car that he knows has some mechanical problems? He never tells you about them because he figures by the time they become apparent the car will be yours, and in the fine print it says once it leaves the lot, they are not responsible for anything that goes wrong.

Lies, lies, and liars are what this country is about. Politicians lie all the time and never keep their word or promises. That's how they are programmed to get ahead. Nothing really gets done, but a politician states that he is lowering taxes and providing more money for education and road repairs, while the budget is in trouble because he bought his wife and children new cars and houses.

So, what happened that I am no longer here? You guessed it! I dared to countermand what Dr. N told Sidney by preparing an unsigned report, telling him the truth about his heart problems, and then went back and mailed reports to three other people that might be alive today if they'd believed what I wrote and what they read.

Living here in this world, those that tell small truths are sentenced to ten days in liar's boot camp to revamp their lying skills, and are fined for their transgressions. Those that dare to tell the whole truth and nothing but the truth are subject to severe penalties, as they are tried in a court of law and sworn to tell a lie; but, of course, they don't. Just how does someone know that they told the truth? Somewhere, where you record your daily lies and your thoughts, sometimes people will add another section in their notebook of what really is the truth, hoping no one will care to read it or notice it. They list it as outlandish lies, but when the incidents are compared and the logs are read by the log overseers each day—and there are many— sometimes they compare notes. And when the truth comes out you are done.

Lies are not so bad if they are not harmful or hateful in context. But when they harm someone, take people's lives by omission because a medical provider does not want the person to unduly worry—that is wrong, and that is the truth, I fear.

Another thing, before I end my tale of pure truth, is that the car salesman sold that car claiming that, even though it was used, it had been tested and test driven for safety precautions. But it was sold in the same condition as when the previous owner brought it in. The result was that the man who bought it was in a serious car accident a few days later because the brakes were worn. He could not stop the car and went onto the side of the road, and the entire front end was demolished and he lost a leg and a hand. Had he known the truth he might have thought twice before buying the car, might have had it tested, and might have had repairs done at his cost or the car company's cost, or bought something else. Truths, when it comes to lives, should be told. Truths when it might be hurtful to someone's feelings? So what if you lie.

What do you think? Lies vs. Truths: Which would you rather hear?

My voice is silenced since I was sentenced to the death penalty for making sure that Sidney knew the truth about his diagnosis before he passed on from this world. His family was shocked, and believe it or not, sided with the doctor, claiming that at least he passed peacefully, not knowing the truth and not suffering. His voice is silenced, yet I wonder what he would say if he could be heard.

There are so many voices that were silenced. There are many more that will follow. But for right now, you, the reader, will decide if all these people deserved their fates or some might have been victims. I lied and I fudged the truth and my soul feels so lonely, and the pain that I inflicted on others by lying haunts me even in death. But maybe the truth if someone is brave or bold enough to tell those I hurt what they really should know will set my soul free so that I can live in eternity in peace.

Silent Voices: Who's Next?

ABOUT THE AUTHOR

Fran worked in the NYC Public Schools as the Reading and Writing Staff Developer for over 36 years. She has three master's degrees and a PD in Supervision and Administration. Currently, she is a member of Who's Who of America's Teachers and Who's Who of America's Executives from Cambridge. In addition, she is the author of three children's books and a fourth that has just been published on Alzheimer's disease in order to honor her mom and help create more awareness for a cure. The title of my new Alzheimer's book is Memories are Precious: Alzheimer's Journey; Ruth's story and Sharp as a Tack and Scrambled Eggs Which Describes Your Brain? Fran is the author of 13 titles and completed by 14th titled A Daughter's Promise. Fran has four titles in her Faces Behind the Stones series and her magazine is MJ magazine. Her next title Silent Voices will be released this July. She was the musical director for shows in her school and ran the school's newspaper. Fran writes reviews for authors upon request and for several other site. Here is the link to her radio show www.blogtalkradio.com, Her network if MJ network on Blog Talk Radio.